Norman Rowland Gale

Cricket Songs

Norman Rowland Gale

Cricket Songs

ISBN/EAN: 9783744767248

Printed in Europe, USA, Canada, Australia, Japan

Cover: Foto ©Andreas Hilbeck / pixelio.de

More available books at **www.hansebooks.com**

CRICKET SONGS

BY

NORMAN GALE

METHUEN AND CO.

36 ESSEX STREET, W.C.

LONDON

1894

THESE CRICKET SONGS ARE DEDICATED TO

ALL RUGBY BOYS IN GENERAL, AND

TO JOHN AND WILLIAM DENTON

IN PARTICULAR

PREFACE

FOUR years ago the author of this book issued a slender volume of cricket songs. Seven of these are now reprinted; the rest are new.

The cricket ball, for the most part, is spoken of as a female. Once or twice the neuter gender is used. *Varium et mutabile semper femina.*

It is hoped that the introduction of the names of prominent players (and one critic) will cause no vexation.

Apologies are tendered to Mr. Moore and Mr. Shakespeare.

CONTENTS

CONTENTS

IN SPRING

GRASS begins to grow,
   Winds to be more civil,
Rollers press the pitch
   For to make it level:
Thrushes pipe a stave
   In the budding thicket;
Snowdrops point to pads,
   Crocuses to Cricket!

A

Soon will stand the Slip
  Crouching for a capture;
Soon the slogger slog
  Fours and fives in rapture!
Soon the curly lob
  Find its love, the wicket;
Snowdrops point to pads,
  Crocuses to Cricket!

Urchins in the road
  Bowl with oblong pebbles,
Sending to each mate
  Bursts of happy trebles:
In the words of slang,
  Summer is the ticket!
Snowdrops point to pads,
  Crocuses to Cricket!

2

UP AT *LORDS*

WHEN Stoddart makes her hum,

Up at *Lords*,

Till the bowler bites his thumb,

Up at *Lords*,

How the Middlesex supporters

Turn vociferous exhorters

As he jumps on Lockwood's Snorters,

Up at *Lords* !

When Stoddart makes her hum

Up at *Lords*,

And my country cousins come

Up at *Lords*

3

With their looks as sweet as honey,

And their exclamations funny,

I am prodigal of money

  Up at *Lords* !

When Stoddart makes her hum

  Up at *Lords*,

And the Surrey Skipper 's glum

  Up at *Lords*,

Oh ! all my odds are even,

And (I hope to be forgiven)

'Tis a truly Cricket Heaven

  Up at *Lords* !

OUT

O VERY potent little word,

      ' Out !'

How often have we sadly heard

      ' Out !'

When stupid umpires surely sin,

Just as to settle we begin,

And say, in place of saying ' in,'

      ' Out !'

Though I am Captain of the team,

      ' Out !'

Though I in doubt may gravely seem,

      ' Out !'

5

Though I have barely scored a run

My average goes down with one,

And other Bats must have the fun—

'Out!'

I see Jones laugh behind his hand—

Out!

Next match, by Jove, the brute shall stand

Out!

Our cousin, Lydia Lake, is here,

And in her eyes I would appear

A Swell; *hinc illae*—Jones's sneer—

Out!

Ah! lucky Jones begins to hit

Out!

Another four!   I wish he'd get

Out!

6

I see him look where Lydia sits

To note if she applauds his hits—

She does !   She 'll burst her gloves to bits !—

   Out !

Yet why should I be Jones's butt,

   Out ?

I have a plan that chap to cut

   Out !

What boots it thus to mope, my soul ?

I go to sit by Lydia.   Scowl,

O Jones, for you, methinks, I bowl

   Out !

LAY ON

ONE wicket to fall and a round fifty runs
Waited for still :
As well to imagine that twice twenty tuns
Go to a jill !
O Jones, be contained if you worship your school,
Block her and snick ;
But punch her to leg if she's handy ; keep cool ;
Lay it on thick !

She comes up full pitch now and then, so look out ;
Dust her along !
And go like a hare if you notice me shout—
Wait for the song !

Tom Emmett will chaff ev'ry chap in the team—

      Jolly old Brick !—

If we funk like young misses of sugar and cream ;

      Lay it on thick !

Go big at those lobs like a lusty old Jones,

      Give it 'em hot !

They break ; get in front with your bundle of bones,

      Leg is the spot !

Take guard. Oh, well banged ! There 's a four to begin,

      See, they are sick !

Another ! Another ! we 're going to win—

      Lay it on thick !

RUB IT IN

It 's all very well
   For Reginald Dibbs,
Who hasn't been hit
   By a ball in the ribs
And one on the shin
   To shout, ' Rub it in ! '

What cheek of R. Dibbs,
   Who, you know, is a sneak,
To scream to you there
   In his high treble squeak,
So strident and thin,
   ' O Jones, rub it in ! '

I wonder if Dibbs,

   When I punch him to-night,

Will think it was wise,

   Or thoughtful, or right,

To caper and grin,

   And yell, 'Rub it in!'

BUZZ HER IN

THEY 'RE running another! Hi, Russell, look sharp!

Buzz her in!

Excuse me, you fellows—a Captain must carp—

Buzz her in!

The fielding's disgusting! when crossing our swords,

Or rather our bats, on the greensward of *Lords*

You *must* loose some few of your muscular cords—

Buzz her in!

Let her come like a flash, and remember, shy straight!

Buzz her in!

We don't want a fourer made into an eight—

Buzz her in!

Suppress all the Extras you possibly can,

For often they total far more than a man—

Just think of last year and the short runs they ran !

Buzz her in !

Don't trot by the side of the ball like a dolt,

Buzz her in !

But cram on the pace like a fine Derby colt,

Buzz her in !

Pick her up, dash her in true and fast to the sticks,

And teach the best batsmen to look to their tricks !

The team that can field well the team is that licks—

Buzz her in !

Get in front of the ball if you can—take the hint—

Buzz her in !

But if she flies past you, why—then you must *sprint* !

Buzz her in !

Turn round in an instant; decide in the same

Which wicket to throw at—it may win the game—

Beware of returns that are timidly tame,

Buzz her in!

Any bruise that you gain in the course of your toil,

Buzz her in!

The Matron will rub with St. Jacob his Oil,

Buzz her in!

And the fellows will cheer when you stop a hot drive—

Thronging round the Pavilion like bees near a hive;

And your name in our annals for ever will thrive—

Buzz her in!

If attention be paid to such details as these,

Buzz her in!

Much trembling will visit the Marlborough knees,

Buzz her in!

Let Rugby's Eleven tremendously try

To catch ev'ry catch be it low, hot, or high;

And down with each overthrow, wide ball, or bye—

Buzz her in !

A COLONIST

The Cornstalk ladles out his Fours
   Or Fivers, as the slog may be.
Oh, how the ring of watchers roars
   When Lyons 's set and Taking Tea !
But when the hitter shows his paces
I like to note the varied faces—

      Shrewsbury's with grief in it,
      George Giffen's with relief in it,
      When Lyons puts his beef in it
         And planks her to the railings !

For Hearne's deliveries are stale,
   And Lockwood's lightning does not thrive ;

16

That fielder's anything but pale

   Who goes great Gunns to stop the drive !

The Nottingham Express ! *He* chases ;

I like to note the varied faces—

     Shrewsbury's with grief in it,

     George Giffen's with relief in it,

     When Lyons puts his beef in it

      And planks her to the railings !

LIGHTNING (GREASED)

Who is Kortright? what is He
   That Lang doth so commend him?
Bowly, fierce and fast is he;
   The heaven such pace did lend him
That he might admired be.

Fast he is, but is he fair?
   For throwing is unkindness.
Those to libel him who dare
   Do only prove their blindness;
And, being kicked, retract it there.

18

Then to Kortright let us sing,

  That Kortright is excelling ;

He excels each rapid thing

  On *Lords* or *Oval* dwelling.

To him let us leather bring.

GOLF STEALS OUR YOUTH

HAVE you seen the golfers airy

Prancing forth to their vagary,

Just as frisky in their gaiters

As a flock of Grecian Satyrs,

Looking everything heroic,

And magnificently stoic,

In a dress of such a pattern

As would fright the good God Saturn ?

Have you heard them curse the sparrow

Fit to freeze your inmost marrow,

When the ball, that should be flitting,

On the grass remaineth sitting ?

Have you watched their cheerful scrambles

In the soft and soothing brambles

While the foe, elate and sneering,

Passes gradually from hearing?

After blaming all the witches,

After rending holes in breeches,

After getting in a muddle

With each rivulet and puddle,

They return, all labour ended,

To record their prowess splendid,

And renew by dictionary

Their fatigued vocabulary.

Let these gentlemen ecstatic,

In their costumes so emphatic,

Crawl to find a rounded treasure

In the horse-pond at their pleasure.

What so good when time is sunny,

And the air as sweet as honey,

As the game of crease and wicket,

England's proper pastime—Cricket?

.

A TOMBOY

THAT long-legged darling, Alice James,
  Plays cricket with the Johnson boys;
A dozen engines could not make
  So shrill a noise.

She 's only twelve, and so, unfrocked
  Beyond her sometimes shameless knee;
And never maiden longed so much
  A boy to be.

She puts on gloves and pads to bat,
  And makes young Johnson bowl her slows.
Good heavens! How she pulled that ball!
  And how she goes!

She's tumbled yards outside the crease,

    And is indisputably out.

Another innings?   Ah, how strong

    That cherry pout!

She keeps on batting all the time,

    And hammers Rupert Johnson's lobs;

She also thumps Emilius's,

    And also Bob's!

So, riding roughshod over rules,

    This long-legged Darling has her will;

And when she's twenty, I expect

    She will do still.

ADVICE GRATIS

If lightning-like you send her down,
   And yet the batsman scores
With here a One and there a Two,
   And then a brace of Fours ;
If calmly confident he stands,
   And makes the leather fly
Past all your slips to dash against
   The boundary palings, why—

      Toss him down a slow, you see,
      He 's sure to have a go, you see ;
      And ten to one the trick is done
      By just a bit of brains, you see !

If round the wicket, medium pace,

    Won't make the batsman budge,

Take special note of what he likes,

    And all his weakness judge.

Suppose he does the leg-glance well,

    Or drives her hot and high,

Or runs to smother each good ball

    And pulls the short ones, why—

        Sling him in a grub, you see,

        A ripping, wicked grub, you see ;

        And ten to one the trick is done

        By just a pinch of wit, you see !

But if with equal craft he meets

    Your wiles, and does not blench ;

If ev'ry bowler in your team

    Desires the restful bench,

And there he stands, the unsubdued,

　With dauntless front and eye,

Prepared to smack your choicest balls

　To realms unheard-of, why —

　　　Don't ask my advice, you see,

　　　No, not at any price, you see ;

　　　But ten to one the trick were done

　　　If I were in your team, you see !

QUINQUAGINTA ANNOS NATUS

OLD Bag and Bat, no more together
  We take the train to Barnes or Tooting;
No more I 'll gallop for the leather,
  Nor grumble when the ball keeps shooting:
I 've fetched her many a handsome clout
  At Rugby, Nottingham, and Dover;
So far Old Time has said ' Not out!'
  But one day he will change to ' Over!'

God bless the grilling days of Cricket!
  They 're gone, but I shall bless them ever,
For good it is to guard a wicket
  By sudden wrist and big endeavour.

Don't think I was a lazy lout

    Who never worked for days of clover;

I earned my games.   Time cries 'Not out!'

    But one day he will change to 'Over!'

Well, I can stand behind the netting

    And watch the 'Coach' so keen and trusty,

Who likes to see the youngsters hitting,

    And teaches them to let out lusty!

I've had my innings, not a doubt,

    And stopped a crack or so at Cover;

I shall not funk when Time says 'Out!'

    And all my watching days are over.

STAR-GAZING

ASTRONOMERS, working like niggers,
Neck-deep in morasses of figures,
From Cricketing vainly would wean us
With diagrams, even of Venus.

We rather would watch a good bowler
Than Bears, be they little or Polar ;
And bar, though of masculine genus,
Wise talk on the Transit of Venus.

When Ladies at *Lords* saunter gaily
With Parsons (not musing on Paley),
Old friend of my boyhood, between us,
Then, *then* is the Transit of Venus !

O BOWLER, BOWLER

O BOWLER, Bowler, when the day is hot,
   Nor any more a wicket you can get;
When Curl and Length and Pace are Gone to Pot
   Before the blade of him serenely set,
IS life worth living—life which only means
   Your ev'ry ball receives stupendous Beans,
And that dread Bat a mighty harvest gleans
   While your Analysis sinks deep in debt?
      He cuts the leather hard and square,
      Nor recks he if it shoots or kicks;
      He sends you clean beyond the screen,
      And lifts you o'er the Baths for six?

31

O Bowler, Bowler, when the Swells all frown

And say your non-success is due to Stodge;

When you in vain invoke the House of Brown

For help the brilliant Batsman to dislodge,

IS life worth living—life which only sends

Reproachful glances from despondent friends,

A varied action and a change of ends,

The subtle slow, the Daisy-cutter's dodge?

The Batsman smacks you to the Courts,

And drives you mad with cunning snicks;

He wipes you clean beyond the screen,

And crumps you o'er the Baths for six!

O Bowler, Bowler, when the Captain calls

'Let Longcroft try,' and places you at Point;

When Cover whispers 'Brown, look out for squalls!'

And, with a vengeance, times are out of joint,

IS life worth living—life which only brings

    Mis-fielding pains and most erratic flings,

Which aid the Batsman's rapid regist'rings,

    But leave you praiseless, slanged and unanoint?

        The Batsman cuts the ball for five,

        Employing judgment, nerve, and tricks ;

        He smites you clean beyond the screen,

        And carts you o'er the Baths for six !

THE CHURCH CRICKETANT

I BOWLED three sanctified souls
    With three consecutive balls !
What do I care if Blondin trod
    Over Niagara Falls ?
What do I care for the loon in the Pit
    Or the gilded earl in the Stalls ?
I bowled three curates once
    With three consecutive balls !

I caused three Protestant ' ducks '
    With three consecutive balls !
Poets may rave of lily girls
    Dancing in marble halls !

34

What do I care for a bevy of yachts,

    Or a dozen or so of yawls?

I bowled three curates once

    With three consecutive balls!

I bowled three cricketing priests

    With three consecutive balls!

What if a critic pounds a book,

    What if an author squalls?

What do I care if sciatica comes,

    Elephantiasis calls?

I bowled three curates once

    With three consecutive balls!

REVENGE

LAST week, when conning Cicero
   In New Big School,
Smith called me, by a paraphrase,
   A senseless mule :
I wasn't sharp enough just then
   To answer, Jack,
That pots had oft been known to call
   The kettles black !

And in the Close the other day
   He called me ' Muff ! '
I think I 've borne his impudence
   Quite long enough !

From length to length abusive men
    Can quickly pass,
So I was hardly staggered when
    He called me ' Ass ! '

But in the nets on Friday eve
    I long did toil
To make old Smith rub in at night
    St. Jacob's Oil !
If on the Smithian shins remains
    An unbruised inch
My name is not Bartholomew
    Ezekiel Finch !

CHUCK HER UP

THE leader was mightily pleased when he saw
That vanguard of his, with their trailing spears,
Stand up from their stoop by a common law
And welcome the sea with a round of cheers !
No doubt that he laughed as he drank his fill
Of the plundered wine in his golden cup ;
But he knew not joy as an English boy
With his summer-time shout—' Chuck her up ! '

And doubtless Columbus by hope deferred,
Wan, weary and worn, was down in the dumps
Till they brought him news of a mainland bird,
And fished up a couple of floating ' pumps.'

38

However polished the Portuguese phrase

That left his lips like a shot from a *Krupp*,

Allowing for dates I find it translates

By our cricketing shout—'Chuck her up!'

How decent when free of each Latin rule

To dash on your whites and rush to the field,

To do or die for the sake of your school

Where many have slogged and many appealed!

You feel in your heart like such chaps as Grace,

Or Surrey's old glory, the steadfast Jupp,

When you yell 'How's that?' to the Umpire, Pratt,

And the oracle says—'Chuck her up!'

'Twas a catch that dismissed the finest foe,

And your Captain hastens to pat your back!

So you modestly call it a fluke, and show

The mark through the glove and the thumbnail's crack:

But *Pater*, watching the match from the tent,

Remembers your wish for a Bernard pup,

And makes up his mind to be extra kind

For the sake of the shout—' Chuck her up ! '

Thus, too, when our Lion is great again,

And roars at the tramp of advancing foes,

You may purchase praise by a twinge of pain

In the midst of battle and giant blows !

And next, when the English Flag's on the hill—

Though many are never again to sup—

For love of your land where the words were planned

Cry out to your men—' Chuck her up ! '

TWO CRITICS

WHEN that I was a little lad
    I dearly loved Amelia James ;
She always seemed sunshiny glad,
    And took such notice of the games !

Selina, who was Acton's pet,
    Distinctly looked prepared to scratch ;
She never stood behind the net,
    And never came to watch a match.

But Miss Amelia took such pride
    In all our study and our sport,
That once I think she nearly cried
    When half our team got out for nought.

She knew the secrets of the slips ;

  And when a friend or foe played well

A cheer came from her kindly lips

  That made a fellow feel a Swell !

We loved to see her freckled face,

  We loved to hear her jolly fun ;

We searched her out a shady place,

  And clapped with her the stolen run.

I loved her most of all the men,

  For Mother's eyes were such a blue ;

I loved her as a boy of ten

  Can love a girl of twenty-two !

One day we played a rival team,

  And I made eighty-four, not out ;

I knew Amelia's face would beam,

  And sometimes heard her pretty shout !

At night the Doctor sent for me

    And said my feat was not amiss ;

Miss James, though, took me on her knee

    And thanked me with a clinking kiss.

BUTTERED

BUTTERED again, by Jingo,

    Buttered again !

Likely to make your lingo

    Awfully plain !

Isn't it rough on the bowler, too,

Doing his level to cram on screw ?

Easiest catches to three of the crew

    Buttered again !

Stoddart dispenses stingo,

    Buttered again !

Likely to make your lingo

    Awfully plain !

Four to the Off and four to the On,

One on the road to, at least, Hong Kong,

One in the air to the ropes is gone—

    Buttered again !

Fate not fit for a dingo—

    Buttered again !

Likely to make your lingo

    Awfully plain !

Bowl you yorker or bowl you a grub,

Cover and Wicket your efforts snub—

Too much salad—Ah, there is the rub—

    Buttered again !

SPARKLING

I 'M not a good Cover I freely admit,
  And I 'm not very handy at Point ;
I 'm growing inert and no longer exert
  The nimble gymnastical joint :
I cannot rejoice when a hurricane cut
  Contuses my shin with its crunch ;
When fielding to hitters my heart patters-pitters,
  But trust me to sparkle at lunch !—
    I radiate freely at lunch.

When Blair puts me Longstop without any pads,
  And delivers occasional Wides,
My thumb is askew, and my bosom is blue,
  And bruises be-smother my sides !

46

I cannot rejoice when a bail comes express

    Saluting my pate with a punch ;

Obesity quivers, there 's wringing of withers,

    But trust me to sparkle at lunch !—

      I radiate freely at lunch.

The National Game is a tonic, I know,

    And a tonic is very good stuff ;

I wish, though, the ball were a little less small,

    And I wish that two pads were enough !

I cannot rejoice when a Richardson comes

    And crumbles me up in a bunch !

I never like tonic behaving cyclonic,

    Preferring to sparkle at lunch !—

      I corruscate freely at lunch.

'DUCK'

WHEN the Doctor pulls up as you pass in the street
> You know he will say :—

'Well, Rogers, I hear that you suffered defeat—
> How many to-day?

Not a hundred, I fear; but you always do well,
> And doubtless you stuck?'

It is hard to admit that you could not excel
> A 'duck.'

For the bowling was easy, the wicket was true,
> And had it not been

That you thought the slow trundler was guilty of *screw*
> You had driven it clean !

How galling to read in the *Sportsman* next day—

    What horrible luck !—

' H. Rogers (the Captain) caught Grinstead, bowled May,

    A " duck." '

But 'tis worse when your Uncle and sweet Cousin Bell

    Come over to watch

All your wonderful deeds as a very great Swell—

    The hope of the match !

And Bell asks your score with a traitorous smile,

    More knowing than Puck ;

And you say (looking straight in her eyes all the while)

    A ' duck.'

But when Fogson, your rival, makes Four after Four,

    And Three after Three,

And next a grand drive, that adds six to his score,

    Right over the tree,

Bell's eyes with excitement delightedly flash—

She praises his pluck !

So you think that the worst of emphatical trash

Is ' duck.'

ON THE SPOT

NOTHING comes amiss,
    Kicker, Shooter, Yorker,
How the Champion bangs
    Lob or cunning Corker!
Let the watchers scold
    Johnny Briggs or Mold,
Censure matters not—
    Grace is on the Spot!

The Champion's on the Spot again
To stop the Gloucester Rot again,
And bowling goes to Pot again
Before the King of Cricket!

Hornby rubs his head,

    Fourer after Fourer !

Now the pace is warm

    Even for the Scorer.

This is simply joy—

    Lump it in, Old Boy !

Don't she travel just ?

    Grace is on the Bust !

The Champion's on the Bust again,

'Tis fine to see him Dust again ;

Don't talk to me of rust again,

    You grand old King of Cricket !

THE HOPE OF SURREY

WHEN Surrey ladled out defeat,

    Who did it?

When Notts and Yorks and Kent were beat,

    Who did it?

    Lohmann did—George Lohmann—

    Something like a yeoman,

    Neither fast nor slow man,

      George!

Surrey wants you—come again!

England wants you—cross the Main!

    Say Good-bye to

    Capetown sky, you

Best of Georges, come again!

Though bowlers good as you should come
(Not likely !)
From you to them shall fancy roam?
Not likely !
Soldier, sailor, tinker,
Ev'ry proper thinker,
Knows you are a clinker,
George !

Surrey wants you—come you back !
England wants you—homeward tack !
Say Good-bye to
Capetown sky, you
Best of Georges, come you back !

May warmer heavens make you whole
For Surrey !

How men would roar to see you bowl

    For Surrey!

  Nurs'd and help'd and mended,

  Truly kept and tended,

  Come and be our splendid

    George!

Shuter wants you home again!

England wants you—cross the Main!

    Say Good-bye to

    Capetown sky, you

George of Georges, come again!

BOMBASTES

In dazzling pads Bombastes went
    To give the bowling Beans ;
He stalked along in sweet content,
    Triumphant in his 'teens.
He launched his muscle at a Slow,
    But heard the timber clink ;
Bombastes homeward sped and said,
    'Whatever do you think?
Bowled by a beastly lob, confound it !
Jumped in too far and hit all round it !
Easy enough to now expound it—
    Bowled by a beastly lob ! '

At luncheon-time Bombastes swore,

    By oaths not one, nor twain,

That he would make the fielders sore

    When he went in again !

A second time the hero strode

    With Allsopp in his head ;

Bombastes missed the first ; he cursed

    Consumedly, and said—

' Bowled by a beastly lob, confound it !

Jumped in too far and hit all round it !

Easy enough to now expound it—

    Bowled by a beastly lob ! '

May ev'ry braggart talking big

    Secure the Double Duck !

By Roman grape and Grecian fig

    I wish him dirty luck !

May underhanded artfulness
   Precipitate his end,
His only comfort be, at tea,
   To moan before a friend—
'Bowled by a beastly lob, confound it!
Jumped in too far and hit all round it!
Easy enough to now expound it—
   Bowled by a beastly lob!'

ENGLAND *V.* AUSTRALIA

THE Champion Grace to the match has gone,
  In the British ranks you 'll find him,
His magic bat he has girded on,
  And his pads are slung behind him !
' Ground of *Lords*,' said the Bearded Pard,
  ' Though all the rest amaze thee,
My stumps for thee I 'll keenly guard,
  One faithful bat shall praise thee ! '

The Champion smacked, and the *Terror's* reign
  Could not bring his wicket under ;
He made the Cornstalk's cunning vain,
  For he smote each ball like thunder !

And said, ' No screw shall baffle me,

Thou soul of bowling bravery,

This game shall prove old England free,

She shall never sink in slavery ! '

CRICKET ON THE HEARTH

WHEN red-nosed Winter takes the road,
   An icicle his walking-stick;
When frost is on the woodman's load,
   And snow is falling fast and thick,
Come, lusty youth and sapless eld,
   Let's make a circle round the blaze
      And talk of stumps,
      Of nasty bumps,
   That flew and came in sunny days.
For Cricket is played again, again,
   At freezing time in Hull or Bath;
When summer's done the game's not gone—
   There's Cricket on the Hearth!

Here's Jones from Rugby, Eton Jack,
  And Grandpapa who, long ago,
Loved hitting when the Field was slack,
  And crumped the bowling, swift or slow!
No more he's nimble on the green,
  But what a history he tells
        Of Surrey men,
        And hits for ten,
  And heaps of most tremendous Swells!
For Cricket is played again, again,
  At freezing time in Hull or Bath;
When summer's done the game's not gone —
  There's Cricket on the Hearth!

The girls may call to Hide-and-Seek,
  And lovely lasses take the floor;
But we discuss the Lob and Sneak,
  The Canvas, Umpire, Over, Score!

How great a game to fill July,

    May, June, and August with delights,

        Yet in the frost

        Be never lost,

    But stir the blood on nipping nights!

For Cricket is played again, again,

    At freezing time in Hull or Bath;

When Summer's done the game's not gone—

    There's Cricket on the Hearth!

DARK BLUE

O STATESMEN who devise and plot
 To keep the White above the Black,
Who tremble when your bolt is shot
 Lest love and loyalty grow slack,
There's not a deed of craftsmanship,
 There's not a thing Red Tape can do,
Shall knit the Hindoo with the Celt
 As much as this—the Cambridge Blue !

No million acres of Despatch,
 No tanks of governmental ink,
Can force a native not to watch
 For days when England's star may sink.

Build factories to weave the tape,
　　Make tables for the rice and dew—
Do all your best, and you shall miss
　　The binding force of Cambridge Blue !

An Indian gentleman to-day
　　Has staled your tortoise policy ;
And thousands cheer to see him play,
　　A splendid batsman, quick and free.
A game shall dwindle all your cares,
　　A clever catch and runs a few !
A Parliament may fail indeed,
　　But not the band of Cambridge Blue !

THE LAST BALL OF SUMMER

'TIS the last ball of Summer
   Left rolling alone;
All his artful companions
   Are smitten and gone;
No trace of his kindred,
   No shooter is seen
To relate all the glories
   Of Briggs and Nepean.

I 'll not leave thee, thou lone one,
   To curl on the stumps;
Since thy brothers were slogged so,
   Partake of their thumps!

Thus kindly I smack thee
  Afar in the heavens,
Where the mates of thy tribe went
  For sixes and sevens!

And soon may there follow,
  Ere sinews decay,
A capital season
  To get thee away!
For muscles must wither,
  Our cricket be flown;
And we shall inhabit
  Pavilions, and groan!